CAN YOU SPOT THESE ROMAN INVENTIONS HIDDEN IN THIS BOOK?

A Roman numeral

A newspaper

A postman

An aqueduct

A codex

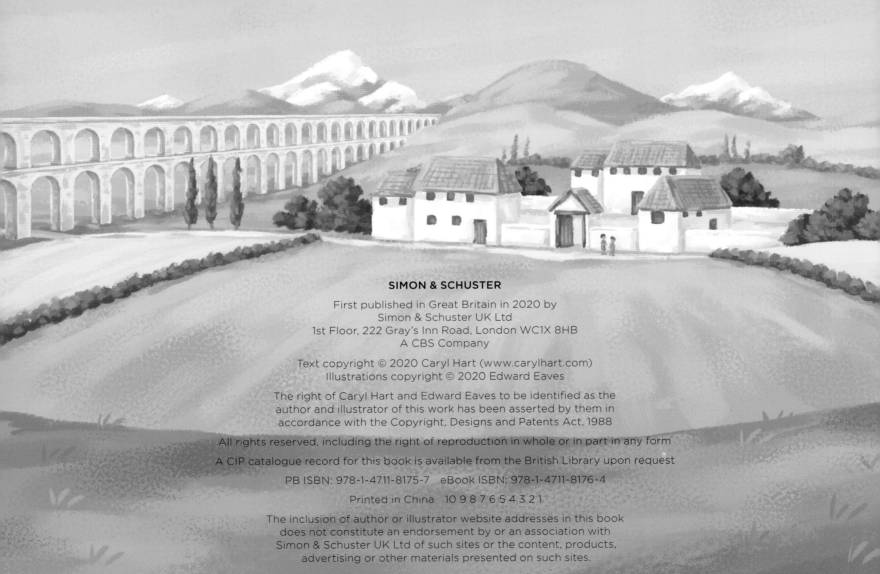

For Ed, whose incredible illustrations
have brought these books to life!

And for ALL the Albie fans out there . . .
we couldn't have done this without you!
CH

For Caryl. Happy 10th Albie Book Birthday! xx
EE

SIMON & SCHUSTER

First published in Great Britain in 2020 by
Simon & Schuster UK Ltd
1st Floor, 222 Gray's Inn Road, London WC1X 8HB
A CBS Company

Text copyright © 2020 Caryl Hart (www.carylhart.com)
Illustrations copyright © 2020 Edward Eaves

The right of Caryl Hart and Edward Eaves to be identified as the
author and illustrator of this work has been asserted by them in
accordance with the Copyright, Designs and Patents Act, 1988

A CIP catalogue record for this book is available from the British Library upon request

PB ISBN: 978-1-4711-8175-7   eBook ISBN: 978-1-4711-8176-4

Printed in China   10 9 8 7 6 5 4 3 2 1

The inclusion of author or illustrator website addresses in this book
does not constitute an endorsement by or an association with
Simon & Schuster UK Ltd of such sites or the content, products,
advertising or other materials presented on such sites.

HOW TO DRIVE A
ROMAN
CHARIOT

CARYL HART   ED EAVES

SIMON & SCHUSTER

London   New York   Sydney   Toronto   New Delhi

It's chilly outside, so I'm playing on my hobby horse.

I'm just brushing
her mane when . . .

"Albie!"

It's Mum.

"How would you like to visit
a real horse?" she says.

A **real** horse? Awesome! I pull on my boots
and we walk along the lane to the farm.

In the field are four horses.
They are gigantic!

"Don't worry," says Mum.
"They're very gentle."

I'm about to give one a carrot when the
sky turns dark and it starts to rain!

We dive into a small barn for shelter. Inside is a girl, holding a great tangle of wool.

"Hello," I say.
"I'm Albie."

"I'm Julia," says the girl. "Are you any good at knots? I'm meant to be knitting socks for my father. He's guarding a big wall in a cold country called Britannia."

I try to help but it just makes things worse! Suddenly, the ground begins to shake.

"Look! It's a parade!" cries Julia.

We stare out of the doorway as lots of golden chariots head up the lane towards us.

"They're on their way to the hippodrome for a big race," says Julia.

A hippo-WHAT?

I step outside to get a closer look but . . .

. . . Something comes flying out from under my feet.
I jump back in fright, and bump into some pots.

AAARGGHH!

Mwwwaaarrrrll!

The noise frightens the horses and they bolt away!

Julia grabs my hand and we
race after the runaway chariot.

"They're heading for the city!"
she shouts. "We have to stop them!"

But the horses are
galloping so fast, it's
impossible to catch up.

"We have to find a shortcut!" I pant.
"Then we can warn everyone
to get out of the way!"

"Good idea!"
says Julia.
"Follow me!"

We duck down an alley and dodge through a maze of narrow streets. I hope Julia knows where she's going!

Quick as a flash, she pulls me through a doorway and . . .

WOOOAHH!

We land right on top of the chariot!

I cling on tightly as the horses gallop out of control.

"We're heading straight for the market!" I cry.

Heellp!

But Julia is not afraid. "I always wanted to be a chariot driver but girls aren't allowed!" she says.

NEWS! CHARIOT RACE TODAY!

Then she grabs the reins and pulls hard to one side.

The horses turn at the last minute, heading away from the market and towards a huge building.

Julia quickly takes control of the horses, but she doesn't make them stop. Instead she spurs them on!

"Where are we going?!" I cry.

"You'll see," Julia grins. "I'm going to show everyone that girls CAN drive chariots!"

We gallop down a long tunnel . . .

. . . and into the hippodrome!

WOAH!

We flash past a blue chariot, then overtake two green
ones! Then the audience jump to their feet with a gasp.

Round and round we race, with the crowd cheering and clapping loudly. There's just one team ahead of us but at the last minute . . .

... we speed up and come in FIRST!!

Hooray!

The Emperor walks towards us, carrying a golden crown but when he sees who we are, he frowns deeply.

"Julia Faustus," he growls. "You know girls are NOT allowed to drive chariots, let alone enter the games!"

"B . . . b . . . but," Julia stammers.

"But," the Emperor continues . . .

"I hear that your actions saved a lot of people from being hurt so I am going to make you an offer."

"If you agree to work in the stables and look after the horses, I will let you begin training to become a real charioteer."

Julia beams with pride. The Emperor smiles and gives me a thumbs up.

"Well done, Julia," I whisper.
"You were amazing!"

"You weren't so bad
yourself," she smiles.